Webster's Coming Home Today

By Joanne A. Reisberg
Illustrated by Tim Williams

Webster's Coming Home Today
By
Joanne A. Reisberg
Illustrated by Tim Williams
Book Design by Whitney Williams

Text Copyright © 2007
Joanne A. Reisberg

Published by
Operation Outreach-USA Press
Natick, Massachusetts

ISBN 978-0-9792144-3-1
ISBN 0-9792144-3-2

Printed in the United States of America

For my sister, Carol, a lover of books
and my husband, Bernie, a lover of animals

Cooper Mattison leaned against the chain-link gate. It had been three weeks since he and mom had dropped off his dog. Would Webster remember him? Would he want to play the same crazy games? What if he had made new friends and didn't want to leave the K-9 Kennel? Cooper's finger traced the silver links in the fence over and over again. "Mom, what's taking so long?"

"Web's being cleaned up," she answered. "If he knew you were waiting he'd probably jump this fence."

Cooper laughed. "That's silly." Cooper hadn't paged through dog books looking for the "perfect" pet. He hadn't even decided on a golden retriever. When he saw Web for the first time he was hiding behind the trunk of a pine tree. He could see only his tail and one paw. Then their eyes met. A warmth had hugged Cooper from deep inside. He knew they belonged together and that they'd be best friends forever and ever.

Loud barks echoed down the long hallway. "Mom did 'ya hear that? It's Webster."

"Coo - - per."

"It's true. I can tell. Listen."

Arf, woof woof. Arf, woof woof.

Mom shook her head. "A bark is a bark."

Cooper knew not to argue. He just listened as a wide smile spread across his face. Mom patted his shoulder. As she knelt, he leaned toward her to get a hug.

"We won't do this again," she said. "I promise."

"Really?"

"Really. Next time we plan a trip we'll take Webster with us."

Cooper turned to stare through the fence. The sound of barks had grown louder. The patter of a dog's paws had started down the tile hallway.

"Here's Webster," the owner of the kennel said, leading a playful golden retriever by a blue leash.

Cooper barely heard the tall man tell about what Web ate. He pushed the gate open and knelt. His fingers itched to wrap around his friend. "Come on Web," he called to the two-year-old.

"Come on, boy."

Webster tipped his head to one side and stared at Cooper. His tail didn't wag.

"Mom, do you think he's forgotten me? Do I look different?"

"Well, you did have your hair cut."

Cooper nodded. "Sure, that's it."

"Give Web a few minutes to get used to you again."

Cooper took the leash from the man. "Let's go home, Web." After a slight tug on his leash, Webster followed him to the car.

Sitting in the back seat with Web, Cooper knew what to do. With a grin he picked up a raggedy toy. "Here's your teddy bear." Web wrinkled his nose, sniffed the toy, and turned to look out the window. "It's your favorite. Don't you want to play?"

Webster didn't answer.

Cooper leaned over and snuggled his dog. Something made him tighten his hold. Web had gained weight. Cooper brushed Web's coat and sniffed. "Mom, Web smells different."

"You would too if you used another kind of soap."

Cooper's hand gently stroked Web's back, trying to understand what was wrong. "I know. You're mad at me, aren't you? I guess I'd be mad too if someone dumped me off at a strange house. Come on pal," he pleaded. "Lick my hand so I know we're still best 'buds'."

Webster shifted under the doggie strap and inched away.

Cooper raised his hand, moving it level with both their shoulders. "Mom, Web's bigger than I am."

His mother's eyes met his in the rearview mirror. "Maybe he grew a bit."

Their car turned the corner on Fairview Lane. By now, seeing all the familiar houses, Web's tail should have been wagging. Those yipping sounds should have started in his throat.

"Cooper, what's bothering you?"

Cooper's bottom lip quivered.

"This isn't Web. This isn't my dog."

His mom pulled into their driveway and shut off the engine. She turned around and leaned an arm over the seat. "Cooper, our problem is that we are all tired from that long plane flight. Can you see Web's collar?"

He glanced at the leather strap around the dog's neck and nodded.

"Tell me what name is on the silver band."

He never thought to check Web's collar. It probably said Goldie, or Laddie Boy, or Sandy. Excited, Cooper reached for the strap.

"Webster Mattison," he whispered.

"We should have had an identification chip implanted," Mom said, sounding a little irritated.

"A what?" asked Cooper.

"It's a microchip the size of a grain of rice that the vet puts under the dog's skin. Usually it's placed between the shoulder blades. All the information about the dog is on it. Kennels and police departments use scanners to read the chips so they can return lost dogs to their owners."

His mom took a deep breath. "I'm sorry Web seems different," she said more gently. "Maybe he doesn't feel good."

"Mom, couldn't we call that kennel? See if they have another golden retriever?"

"You've read Web's collar. Please, Cooper, I don't want to hear anymore talk about this dog not being Webster."

Cooper stood inside the back door and unhooked Web's leash. He waited for him to run off. But *this* Web didn't move.

He didn't head to the kitchen for a drink of water.

He didn't even race to the window to watch Mrs. Bellinie's poodle prance around in the next yard.

Instead, he looked as if he were seeing these rooms for the very first time.

"Mom, look. This Web's got a tiny scar on his left hind leg. Our dog doesn't have a scar."

"Cooper, I've got three weeks of washing to do. Web probably cut himself chasing after a playmate at the kennel. Give him a few days and he'll be back to normal."

"Come on...Pal," Cooper said choosing the easiest name he could think of. The dog followed him into his bedroom. A dull thud pounded in Cooper's chest. He closed his eyes and took a deep breath. It was true. No matter what his mom said, this golden retriever belonged to someone else.

Cooper stopped feeling sorry for himself and patted the window bench. "Come on up." As the the retriever jumped onto the padded seat, Cooper's arms slipped around the dog's neck. He laid his head against the soft furry coat and held him as he used to hold Webster. "You miss your best friend, don't you?" Tears trickled down Cooper's face as he thought about Web being with strangers. "I know you do 'cuz I miss my best friend too."

The change was slight but Cooper felt it. Pal turned and began to lick Cooper's neck. "Don't worry. It's up to us now. We have to try and find our friends."

Cooper tugged the hem of his shirt loose from his jeans and used it to wipe his face. He glanced out the window. Across the next block, and that vacant field, was the K-9 Kennel. Sometimes he and Web would watch dogs running around in that fenced-in playground. "Tomorrow, Pal, we'll get some exercise and take a walk by that fence."

The next morning Cooper heard playful barks as he and Pal ran through the tall weeds in the vacant lot. Off in the distance he could see dogs of all sizes scampering inside that fence. And then he saw a golden retriever on the far side of the yard.

"Web," he shouted, jumping over a fallen log. "It's me, Cooper."

A brownish terrier and a long-haired dog stopped in their tracks and stared at him. "Web," he yelled again. But as he reached the fence he knew the dog wasn't Webster.

He heard a whooshing noise and saw the older Bellinie kid hosing down the dog runs. "Hey, Ryan."

"Hi, Cooper.

What's Web's problem?"

How could he say the kennel gave them the wrong dog when his mom didn't even believe him? He glanced down at his new friend. *Friend.* "Web made friends with a golden retriever at the kennel last week. Think he's still here?"

"I remember that dog. Could have been a twin of Web's. His owner picked him up last night."

It's Web!

"Do those people live around here?" Cooper asked.

Ryan shrugged his shoulders. "They were only here three days. Traveling across country, I guess."

Cooper's stomach churned with a new fear. Web could be a gazillion miles away by now. As Ryan and the dogs went inside, Cooper leaned against the fence. Minutes ago he had seen something that puzzled him. It was about those two dogs; that brownish terrier and the long-haired one.

"Yes," he whispered, bending down and ruffling Pal's fur. "Those dogs weren't wearing collars! That's how you got Web's. The people mixed them up when they gave you baths."

Without thinking what he'd say, Cooper grabbed Pal's leash. He ran the length of the fence to the building's entrance. Once inside, he stood in front of the green metal desk until the woman looked up. "My dog stayed here for three weeks," Cooper blurted out.

"I recognize your dog. Hi there, Webster," she said with a smile that didn't look real.

"But this dog isn't Web!"

"Hmmmm," she said reaching for his collar. "It says Webster Mattison right here."

"The collars got mixed up when someone took them off."

Her eyes flashed. "Took them off?" she said, raising her voice. Cooper took a quick step back. "Little boy, these dog collars are never taken off."

Before he could tell her what he'd seen, she reached for the phone.

Cooper headed out the door with Pal trailing behind. He crossed the vacant lot and spotted his mom sitting on their back steps. The way she held her head told him he was in deep trouble. And he knew why. "That lady called you, didn't she?"

His mom nodded. She slid her hand across his shoulder. "I've been thinking. You and Webster are the closest of friends. You know him better than anyone. If you say this dog isn't Web, I believe you."

It took a minute for Cooper to say what was deep inside his heart. "Pal's a nice dog, mom, but he's someone else's dog."

"Okay, I agree. But you're not to go to the kennel and accuse them of giving us the wrong dog until we have proof. Do you understand?"

Cooper nodded.

A week later, Cooper had that proof.

Cooper took Pal to the pet store on Monday and let him pick out his own toy.

On Tuesday he made a new bed for his new friend.
The next day Cooper gave Pal a bath.

It was when he scrubbed Pal between his shoulder blades that Cooper's heart skipped a beat. He felt something that made him stop. His thumb brushed the same spot again and again. There, under the skin, Cooper's finger pressed what felt like a tiny grain of rice. It was just like what Mom had described. He knew what he had found: an identification chip.

"When the K-9 Kennel scans your chip it will prove you're not my dog. We'll find out your name and who owns you." Pal tilted his head like he understood. Cooper reached for a towel knowing what else it meant. Maybe today Webster would finally come home.

Together they raced into the living room. "Mom," Cooper shouted. "Guess what?"

Isabel, his teenaged neighbor, sat on the couch doing her summer school homework.

"Your mother's at a luncheon meeting, Cooper, remember?"

He nodded. Now he'd have to wait a whole hour before she got home. But there was something else he remembered too. His mom had said he couldn't go to the kennel *until they had proof.* He grinned. Well, he didn't have to wait after all.

Isabel kept looking at him. "Anything you want to tell me, Cooper?"

"No, just...just that we're going to take a walk by that vacant lot."

Pal followed at his heels as they ran through the weeds toward the K-9 Kennel.

Once inside the building, the same woman stopped them with a raised hand and a big frown. "Something you forgot last time?"

Cooper chose his words carefully. "Do you have that scanner thing that can read ID chips?"

Her frown deepened. "Of course. Come here with your dog."

Cooper kept his smile inside. He tried but couldn't see when she moved the scanner over Pal's neck. "Does it tell you a name?" he asked.

"No, only an identification number." She turned toward the desk. "We keep all our customers' numbers on file. I have their names right here."

Cooper wanted her to hurry. To tell him Pal's real name and the phone number of the people who had Web.

She looked from her files to Cooper and then back to the papers. "The ID chip says the dog is, let's see. Yes, here it is…um…Webster Mattison. Address, 3630 Fairview Lane. He belongs to Cooper Mattison." Still looking at the file she said, "That's you, isn't it?"

Cooper stared at the woman. She turned away to put the papers into the file and didn't look back at him. His grip tightened on Pal's leash, not believing what he had heard. But she had said their address, his name and Web's. He gritted his teeth. Quietly he motioned for Pal to follow him.

Cooper kicked at the tall grass as they started through the field. Had he been wrong all along? He glanced at the golden retriever walking by his side.

Could this really be Web? His own dog that he didn't recognize?

"You act different," he said patting Pal's back. "You weigh more and

... and you don't remember our games or that jumping trick with the rope. You can't be Web because," Cooper stopped as the reason burst into his brain.

Angry, he turned toward the K-9
Kennel.

"You're wrong," he
shouted,
"because my Web
doesn't have a chip!"

They sat on the front steps together; Cooper with his arm around Pal, Pal with his head on Cooper's shoulder. "That kennel lady didn't fool us. My mom will take us to the police station. They have scanners and then we can get your real name and address." Cooper gave him a hug. "It hasn't been easy for you, but soon you'll be home. You'll eat the kind of dog food you're used to and play with your own toys."

Pal's ears perked up.
"What is it, Pal? What do you hear?"
Cooper searched the yard for a squirrel. He
scanned the driveway. Then he heard it too.

"Arf,
woof,
woof."

He squinted against the bright sun. Off in the distance he saw something at the end of the block. A scruffy looking dog limped down the sidewalk. A broken leash dragged by his side. His fur was filthy and matted. But as he ran, sunlight caught a few strands of golden hair.

Cooper leaped off the steps. His feet pounded the sidewalk as he ran toward the dog. "Webster," he shouted fighting back tears, "is it really you?" He saw his bleeding front paw, the dazed look in his eyes, and knew he'd been traveling for hours.

Cooper dropped to his knees. In seconds, Webster collapsed in his arms.

Pal greeted his friend with happy barks. He trotted alongside as Cooper struggled to carry Web home.

It was after Web had been held, cleaned, and both dogs fed, that Cooper remembered the collar he'd taken off. He studied the printed words on the leather band and sounded out the name. With a grin he looked over at Pal.

"Hey ...Griffin," he called out.

Pal stopped running. He stood perfectly still, his ears on alert.

"Griffin's a great name for you." Griffin smiled a big slobbering doggie smile. His tail wagged. With new energy he bounded across the yard to play.

Soon, the three watched Cooper's mom pull into the driveway.

Together they celebrated with doggie treats and ice cream bars. Then Cooper grew serious. "Mom, I don't want them to mix up any other dogs."

She nodded and gave him a tight hug. "We'll do everything we can to see that it doesn't happen again."

Cooper sat on the kitchen floor between the two golden retrievers. He held the phone in one hand and Griffin's dog collar in his lap. "Double check the number before you press the buttons," his mom said.

Cooper reread the area code. It was the same one as theirs. "Okay guys, here we go." And then he began to dial.

He heard one ring. Two rings. Three rings.

"Hello," an unhappy voice answered.

"This is Cooper Mattison. Is this..." Cooper glanced at the collar again, "is this Shawn?"

"Yes?"

"Well," Cooper couldn't keep the excitement out of his voice, "I've got your dog, Shawn. I've got Griffin."

"Mom!" he heard Shawn scream over the phone. "Somebody found my dog."

Cooper handed the phone to his mom to get directions. He knew exactly how Shawn felt because he had just found his friend.

With a huge grin he leaned over and hugged both dogs.

Today, Webster had finally come home.

About Operation Outreach-USA

Operation Outreach-USA (OO-USA) provides free literacy and character education programs to elementary and middle schools across the country.

Because reading is the gateway to success, leveling the learning field for at-risk children is critical. By giving books to students to own, confidence is built and motivated readers are created. OO-USA selects books with messages that teach compassion, respect and determination. OO-USA involves the school and the home with tools for teachers and parents to nurture and guide children as they learn and grow.

Operation Outreach-USA Press publishes all new materials used in this program.

Children in schools in all fifty states have participated in the program due to the support of a broad alliance of corporate, foundation, and individual sponsors.

To learn more about Operation Outreach-USA and how to help, visit:

www.oousa.org or call 1-800-243-7929